The Story Behind the Mask

by

Tarey Denise

MEEK & HUMBLE PUBLISHING

Mask: a covering for all or part of the face, worn as a disguise to conceal one's identity; a false face

DISCLAIMER

This is a work of fiction. Any references to real people, events, establishments, organizations, or locales are intended only to give the work a sense of reality and characters, businesses, places, events and incidents are either the products of the author's imagination or used in a fictitious manner. Any resemblance to actual persons, living or dead, or actual events is purely coincidental.

THE STORY BEHIND THE MASK

Copyright © 2019 by Tarey D, Meeks
McKinney, Texas 75069

ISBN 978-0-9978878-4-6

Cover Design by Shanetta J'amere
Book Interior and E-book Design by Amit Dey | amitdey2528@gmail.com

Published in McKinney, Texas by **Meek & Humble Publishing**

Library of Congress Cataloging-in-Publication Data:

Meeks, Tarey, 1963 -

Unless otherwise noted, all Scripture quotations are from *The Holy Bible, King James Version.* Copyright © 1977, 1984, by Thomas Nelson Inc., Publishers.

This book and other Meek & Humble Publishing titles can be found and purchased at www.tareydenise.com

Printed in the U.S.A.

Table of Contents

Introduction. v

Chapter One - The Breaking Point 1

Chapter Two - The Next Step 5

Chapter Three - A Way Out. 7

Chapter Four - Write the Vision, Make it Plain 11

Chapter Five - A New Beginning 15

Chapter Six - Step by Step 19

Chapter Seven - Confusion in the Camp. 25

Chapter Eight - The Turning Point 29

Chapter Nine - Identity Crisis. 35

    Mother's Baby, Daddy's Maybe. 35

    Shades of Blackness. 38

    Ball of Confusion 41

Chapter Ten - Eyes Wide Open. 45

Chapter Eleven - A New me in Town 53

Chapter Twelve - Hope for Tomorrow 57

Chapter Thirteen - Growing Pains 61

Chapter Fourteen - Full Circle 65

From the Author 69

Introduction

We all have worn masks at some point in our lives in some capacity. For years, I hid behind masks believing that the images they portrayed were more appealing than the real me. One thing I failed to realize was that every unpleasant situation or roadblock I encountered, compelled me to add another mask. That's right, I was not just wearing one mask but a layer of masks. This practice began to weigh me down so much that I couldn't move forward; no matter how hard I tried. The day I surrendered to God, began a transforming process where the layers of masks were removed one by one. The Lord likened my journey to the metamorphosis of a butterfly. As the butterfly goes through several stages to become what it is destined to be, so did I. Four stages complete the butterfly's life cycle: the egg, the larvae, the chrysalis, then the butterfly. In each stage, there are a certain set of strengths, weaknesses, and struggles that are revealed, acknowledged, and then, conquered. I can honestly say that my process was no different. Some moments were more painful than others. Staring at myself in the mirror, totally naked, being face to face with everything I believed to be ugly about myself was the hardest thing I have ever done. However, it was the most necessary. As my desire to seek God and to be in His will grew, He began to uproot those things in me that were not like Him and that were not beneficial to where He was taking me. Those things literally had me in bondage. In each trek of my journey, there was a form of stripping, breaking, smashing, and molding that took place, some deeper and harder than others, but nonetheless, vital to my transformation. Sometimes, I wanted to cry, turn around and give up; but the Holy Spirit, my comforter, would not let me give in. He was constantly reminding me of how far I had come, and that God wouldn't bring me this far to leave me. He would give me glimpses of the promise, and I hung on because of the promise. I hung on because of God's word about the promise. I hung on because God is not a man that He should lie. I hung on because I knew that God would bring me through. I am so grateful to know God, my Father, on this level. I am so blessed to have this ever-evolving relationship with Him. I knew about Him as I was growing up, but now I have gained this intimate, firsthand knowledge of who He is. Through this revelation, I have come to know who I am. I am the beloved of Christ, His daughter, who is fearfully and wonderfully made in His image. I can look back now and see that everything I went through was worth the result. Lives were changed, families and relationships were restored, strongholds and yokes were broken, all because God chose me to be the catalyst for His plan. He gave me wisdom to make the right choices. He gave me strength to endure to the end. He gave me the courage to be obedient and write *"The Story Behind the Mask"*.

~Tarey Denise~

Chapter One

The Breaking Point

One night in March of 2013, I was alone, lying in silence. The only light in the room came from a full moon, peeking through my curtain less window. I began to stare up into the sky, straight through the clouds trying to see past the stars wondering where is this "God" that is supposed to love me so much? Is He really out there? Does He know how broken my heart feels right now? Why in the world does He allow me to keep coming to this lonely place? I don't think I can take this anymore. If I wasn't at my breaking point, I was certainly on the verge of it. It was so quiet this night that I could almost hear my tears hitting my pillow as they streamed down my face. I could feel that my eyes were swollen from crying so much, I probably didn't look like myself.

Have you ever looked in the mirror and wondered, "who is this stranger looking back at me?" Isn't that a scary feeling? The person who you once thought you were or thought you should have been is not the exact representation of what you see before you. This is what can happen after years of pretending that all is well. Trying to convince others that you are satisfied with the events that have taken place in your life can be exasperating. Covering up your shortcomings, making excuses, and sinking down to blaming others becomes very taxing; even for the best of us. Every wrong decision would be covered with yet another mask. Why is it that we don't ever want to admit that we have failed at something? Why does the world expect us to be perfect when the Word of God clearly tells us that "not one is perfect"? For whatever reason, we continue to believe the lies of the enemy and we keep putting on the pretense that we've got it all together. After so many years of working so hard to conceal our humanness, the weight of the masks get so overwhelmingly heavy that we crash.

That is what happened to me that night. My life had fallen apart right before my eyes and the world didn't even see it coming. I had been functioning like the walking dead for months, probably much longer, and not a soul came to comfort me. No one recognized that I wasn't myself. I wore my masks very well. I had worn them so long that when it all came crashing down, I didn't even recognize myself. So here I am alone in this room, crying and crying until I was empty. Up to this point, I had done all that I knew to do about my situation, and I hadn't gotten any results. As a matter of fact, things were probably the worst that they could get. Truth be told, my husband had moved out almost a year prior to this day and we had been keeping it a secret. For months, we played the game. I only stayed in the game for hopes that at some point, we would win. This night though, I was ready to throw in the towel. I had prayed, I had fasted, I had friends praying, I pleaded, I cried, I fought, I cussed … at the end of all that, I got nothing. I had no clue how I had gotten to this place. I had no answers for why my husband didn't love me anymore. I couldn't find a reason why I was always misunderstood. I'm wondering, where is this God that is supposed to love me so much? Why can't I feel Him? Why can't I hear Him? As I lay on the futon, I gazed out of the window looking past the clouds, moon and stars straight up to heaven. "God, where are you when I need you?" I cried. "I can't do this anymore!" Suddenly, I heard a voice speak, "Tori, *my daughter. I've been waiting on you.*" I sat up and looked around the room to make sure no one had walked in on me. Did I just hear God's voice? I was still alone in the room, so it had to be. I had heard God. I sat still waiting for more. I needed to make certain that it was the voice of God that I heard. The next thing I heard caught me off guard. I heard *"Move as if your life depends on it!"* The voice was stern and direct. It wasn't a request; it was a command.

Now I don't know about anyone else's experiences with hearing and recognizing God's voice, but I sure was thinking why the first thing I clearly hear God telling me to do is move. Hearing God say move, only brought more questions to my mind. When? How? Where? I had been fighting this battle for a long time and could not get a victory. I was constantly tapping out with no one to hand the baton to. I knew about God and had only heard about having a personal relationship with Him, but I really couldn't grasp how to do so. I didn't know how to let go and let God. I didn't know how to give it to Him. After hearing Him speak to me that night made me realize that in this next phase of my life, I was going to need Him and I would have to stay close. I would have to figure it out just what those words meant. I also concluded that the only way I would get through it, would be for God to send someone to literally take me by the hand.

Chapter Two

The Next Step

*H*earing God tell me to move like my life depended upon it was real to me. I knew in my heart exactly what I had to do. I know that in the last year or so, I had sunk so low that I was definitely an easy prey for the enemy. I honestly don't know where the thoughts in my mind would have led me if God had not interceded when He did. I had always heard that God may not come when we want Him, but He's always on time. I thank God that His word is true.

Wherever God was going to lead me, I knew that I had been given another opportunity to get a grip on my life before it spinned out of control. As I think back to this day, God already had everything figured out for me. All of the events up to this point were preparing me for this day, this moment.

As I said earlier, I had been seeking to know God in an intimate way but could never get there. Now I'm feeling as if I was on my way. I haven't heard God speak to me since that night, but I have had the feeling that someone was watching over me. My spirits were definitely lifted, and I was very excited about what was about to take place. Whatever that was.

Chapter Three

A Way Out

There was one relative of mine that God had given me a special connection with. It went far beyond what's encompassed in our DNA. She had a relationship with God that I wanted to understand. She was the person that I would go to when things got complicated. Whenever my kids and I needed to get away, her door was always open to us. Yeah, I spent a lot of time running from my situation because that was what I knew to do. I didn't know how to handle what I was dealing with. Marriage wasn't easy and I couldn't figure out why this man God gave me to was acting out.

Isn't that how we do? We always place the blame on the other person and never acknowledge our role in the dysfunction. "So and so made me do it"; or "if you wouldn't have done this, then I wouldn't have done that". That is nothing but a cop out. Soon enough, I would be getting a rude awakening.

Anyway, back to my relative. She would pray with me, cry with me and took the time to try to lead me to Jesus. You know, there's an old saying that you can lead a horse to water, but you can't make him drink. Well, just call me a horse. In all my getting, I just didn't understand. That didn't stop her though. She never gave up on me. There were times when she would just call me out of the blue to talk and before the conversation was over, she had ministered to me just what I needed. That's the connection I was talking about.

The night God spoke to me, I had a vision. It was Michael Jackson's Billy Jean video. I saw Michael taking steps over square tiles and as he stepped on each tile, one by one, it lit up. God said, *"You must trust me and go where I say go. This is how I am going to lead you, one step at a time."* I wasn't going to see anything ahead of the step I was on. This was going to truly be a test of my faith. I was on a crash course and my only objective was to pass. I was about to throw all caution to the wind and trust God with my life. Why not, it was His anyway.

Two days after my encounter with God, I received a call from my relative. I was at work and took a short break to catch up with her. After a point in the conversation, she said, "Tori, the Lord has told me that I have to take you hand in hand, step by step through this thing." My God is so amazing. You see what I was talking about; the connection. I dropped the phone and ran around the office. Once I calmed down reality began to set in. I didn't know what I was going to do or how I was going to do it. I do know that I had to do something. I don't think I slept too good that night, which was no different from the past 300 nights, except the fact that instead of crying, I was thinking of a master plan because God had given me a way out.

Chapter Four

Write the Vision, Make it Plain

The following weekend, I took a trip to visit my daughter who was in college at Spelman. While I was there, we decided to travel to visit my relative. It was only a 2 ½ hour drive from where we were. She was glad to see us and I was definitely glad to see her. She had invited us to attend a prayer service with her and I figured that was just what I needed. It was an awesome experience and I definitely felt the presence of God there. In the midst of the spirit flowing, a prophetic word came forth for me. I had never met the gentleman before this night and here it is he's telling me that God said it's time to move like my life depended on it; and within the next three (3) weeks. I know that I had heard this before. I knew it was God. Now all I had to do was trust Him. When my daughter and I made it back to Atlanta, I didn't sleep for the next three days. Instead,

I was up praying and thinking and trying to calculate my next move. I was saying, Lord your word says I can trust you, but can I trust you? I was scared.

When I made it back to Louisiana, I knew what I had to do. I didn't tell anyone of my plans yet. Maybe I was hoping that I wouldn't have to leave. I was really wondering how I was going to tell my husband. We were already living separately even though we made appearances together, like at church and family functions. (insert mask here) We were definitely estranged although I had never admitted it or spoken it out of my mouth. Anyway, that Sunday after church, my husband was driving me home. I asked if he would move back home so we could try to work things out together. There I was, trying to help God. But God already knew what was about to happen. My husband said, "Well, Tee" (I liked when he called me Tee, lol) "Tee, I know you're trying to get right with God and I have all of this stuff going on and I don't want to mess you up. When I come back home I want to be right so we can move forward." Thank you Lord for that response, because if he would have said anything different I wouldn't be where I am today.

When I got to work the next day, I went to my supervisor and told her that I was thinking about resigning and would let her know for sure by the next day. She said she understood and that I should pray and make sure it was God. That evening after work, my husband picked me up from work. Our conversation was minimal, if any, and like usual, he dropped me off and went on about his business. Well, that next day, I had my resignation papers typed up signed and ready to go. My supervisor and I waited until the end of the day to tell my coworkers my news. I had done it. There was no turning back now. But that wasn't the hardest part. Now I had to tell my family, including my husband. I was nervous about that. I didn't know how he was going to react. I didn't know if he was even going to care. My earliest opportunity came the following day. We had attended bible study and this time we drove in separate cars. During bible study, I leaned over to him to tell him I needed to speak to him before he left. After study, he came over to my car and got in beside me. I started by saying that I would respect his wishes of giving him time to get himself together. I then said, "I'm not asking for a divorce, but I need you to do the same for me." I told him that I had resigned from my job and was moving. He burst into tears. That really surprised me. I think I caught him off guard. I told him I just needed time away to allow God to work on me. Now if that was the hand he fanned with, I'm not sure, but he quickly recovered, accepted my decision and gave me his blessing. Two weeks later, my truck was loaded to capacity and I was beginning my journey.

Chapter Five

A New Beginning

I'm on the highway, heading to a new beginning. I did not imagine that this is what I would be doing in my 50th year of life. I'm thinking that I wanted a relationship with God and that I wanted to change my life, but this was not quite what I was expecting. Nonetheless, I was feeling a little lighter about my shoulders, like a load had been lifted. Yes, that's it. I can move my shoulders and neck a little better now. I think I feel a smile creeping up on my face. Wow. When God makes moves in your life, it will have your head spinning. He's so amazing. At this moment, I don't feel any fear, just excitement about what's ahead of me. I remember when I was getting divorced from my husband. (oh yeah, my husband and I had been married in 1989, then divorced in 1997, then remarried in 2002) To end up in this place again was so disheartening. When I was filing the paperwork for the divorce, I had convinced myself that it was what I wanted, but when I got those signed documents in my hands stating the divorce was final, I cried like a baby. I cried so much, I had to leave work and go home. That's the initial feeling I was having on that drive. I just pray that I don't have any regrets like back then.

After many hours of driving, singing, and praising and constant calls from my relative asking me "where you at na?", (in her southern Louisiana accent) I finally made it to her house. She was outside waiting on me. Her excitement made me feel that much better about what I was getting into. Her kids came out to greet me with hugs and big smiles and all I could do was smile in my heart and tell God thank you.

It didn't take long to get settled in. Everybody gave a hand in unpacking my things. I was set up in my own bed-room. That's right, they were happy that I had chosen to be with them and made me feel at home. I had visited with them before, but somehow, they knew this time would be different.

After receiving all the love and hugs and my things were unpacked, I was alone in my room. The excitement slowly began to fade away. Reality was trying to rear its ugly head into my perfect new life. I started asking myself, "girl, what were you thinking?" Did I move too quickly? "Was that really God speaking to me?" Bad enough I had family and friends back home thinking I had gone crazy, now I'm thinking it myself. I began to doubt that I had even heard

God. I didn't even really have that kind of relationship with God where He would even speak to me let alone send me hundreds of miles away from all that I knew. I cried, "Lord, what have you gotten me into?"

Isn't it just like the enemy to come and bring doubt into your mind? There's one thing you should always remember about the enemy and it is that he is always on his job. He's always looking for a way to disturb the peace. I'm thinking, maybe I won't have to be here that long. Maybe my husband will have this great revelation and we will live happily ever after…... NOT!

Chapter Six

Step by Step

I t wasn't until I arrived at my new destination that I realized I was weighing in at 205 pounds. I can't tell you when it happened, but it seemed like I just woke up like that. I hadn't realized just how far into depression I had gone. I wondered how much of the weight was spiritual and not so much of my overeating. I knew that I had gotten into a routine of going to work and coming home and getting straight in the bed. I had grown so tired of dealing with "my issues" that I just didn't want to fight anymore. All the pretending I had done throughout the years, had caught up to me. At times it seemed that I was on my way to getting a breakthrough only to get caught back up in the same vicious cycle again. I couldn't win for losing. The night God spoke to me, I think I cried for 7 hours straight. I went from crying to gasping for breath to asking God why me. I just couldn't understand why I was going through what I was going through. What did I do to deserve this? I was trying to replay every wrong thing I had done in my life, to see if it made sense. The funny thing about that is I couldn't recall too much of my past. I could only remember snippets of events. Most of them that I could think about were things that I was told as I got older. Maybe I had done something that was so bad that I had blocked it out. I came to realize that things that happened in my past had a direct correlation to what I was dealing with in my present.

Of course, you can imagine that I didn't sleep too well that first night. Upon waking the next morning, I told God that He had to reinforce his instructions in a way that I knew that I was in the right place, both physically and spiritually. I got dressed and decided to tag along with my relative as she walked her kids to school. It's at the end of March, so the weather was just right for walking; not too cold and not too hot. It was a good walk and I think the breeze did me some good. When we made it back to the house, we both went to freshen up from the walk. We then met at the kitchen table and she presented me with a book. When I read the title, all I could do was look up and say thank you Jesus. The name of the book was "Just enough light for the step I'm on: Trusting God in the tough times" by Stormie Omartian. That was amazingly the same thing God had told me before I left. The kitchen table became our morning meeting place. We would pray, read and share our perspectives on what we read. I really looked to her to help shed some light on what I was going through. She definitely had taken me by the hand to walk me through this thing. From that experience, I began journaling my thoughts and prayers and even wrote some poetry about my newfound relationship with God. Any questions that I had, I brought back to her the next time we met. Sometimes we would get some insight from her husband, an awesome, anointed Man of God that I totally respect. He is truly a man after God's own heart and one of great faith; and I honestly mean GREAT faith. He made serving God look easy, but I came to know that it takes great dedication and determination. Along with our daily ritual of meeting at the table, we incorporated a daily walk to the park. It was during some of those walks that we had our deepest conversations about my situation. Some of the conversations made me think and some made me angry, but they were all necessary. We discussed my marriage, my relationship with God, my friendships, my children and my goals and aspirations. By the time we got back to the house, we were ready to hear from God. We would pray, read, cry, talk, laugh and sometimes just worship. For the next two months, this is what God had me doing. By the time we finished the book, I was coming to understand more and more of WHO God was as opposed to just knowing ABOUT Him. It was becoming evident just what God was expecting of me and just how I was supposed to get it done. I had even lost 10 lbs.

One morning my relative didn't meet me at the table. I got dressed and was ready to get started but she didn't come out of her room. I went back to my room and waited for a while, then went back to check for her, but still her seat at the table was empty. I went back to my room and turned on the TV. I sure was wondering what was going on with her. A few hours later she came to my room, still in her robe saying she wasn't feeling so good. I told her I understood and that I hoped she felt better. I don't think we met at all that week. By this time, my little brain had conceived several different scenarios of what was really going on. (Yeah I forgot to mention that I think a lot. My husband used to complain that I drove him crazy with stories I would come up with about what he was doing and who he was doing it with. He would say that it was all in my mind.) I was wondering if she was thinking that this was too much for her; if I was becoming a nuisance; was she tired and just didn't want to do it anymore. Needless to say, I had thought so much about what was going on in her mind and the real reason why we were not meeting, that I had packed my bags to take a trip to Atlanta by my daughter. I made myself so uncomfortable with my thoughts and just had to get away. I didn't even tell her that I was leaving but she came to my room and saw my bags packed. I told her I was going to see my daughter for a few days. She and her husband walked me outside and watched me pack the car. She said, "girl, you're not coming back." I told her don't be silly, I'll be back.

It's now the end of June, and I'm still in Atlanta. As a matter of fact, for the last couple of days, I had been apartment hunting. It looks like my relative was right. I wasn't going back. I can look back now and see what having a simple conversation could have prevented. I don't understand why it was so difficult for me to express myself to her at that time. Instead, I did the usual and came up with my own story and conclusion.

I finally found an apartment that I liked that was reasonably priced and not too far from my relative. My daughter and I drove to Columbus to make the deposit. While there, we stopped in on my relative. I was glad to see her and she seemed happy to see me too. Mind you, I'm still in my crazy mindset. We talked a bit and we gradually got around to talking about when I left. She explained to me that God had directed her to pull back so I could make the initiative. God wanted to know that I was sincerely seeking Him. He wanted to know exactly what my determination level was. He wanted me to come after Him, not for Him to be delivered to me at the table. That was deep. I totally understood. God was becoming so real to me.

Chapter Seven

Confusion in the Camp

I moved into my apartment on July 12, 2013. I was so excited. I spent the next few weeks decorating, shopping and ordering things online. I was going to make my place so beautiful that everybody was going to love it. After it was all done, I was in my beautiful place....... ALONE.

My relative and I kind of picked back up where we left off. I would get up early and drive over to her house and the day would begin. We continued our daily walks and fellowship at the table. We would do some shopping and talking and sharing. We were determined to deepen our relationship with God and to get a better understanding of this life as a believer. She was an awesome mentor and she was definitely walking me through. I thought back to her telling me her instructions to lead me to Him. I knew that I was on my way. I had gotten to a point when I could read something in the bible and get clarity about what God was revealing to me. Sometimes I was able to see how it pertained to my present situation. I was beginning to feel good about where God had taken me because I was seeing a change in myself; for the better.

During the last few months of 2013, we began to really bond. I was always looking forward to our conversations and I hung onto every word that she said. It seemed that every issue I had, I went to her to get my answer. I wanted to know her opinion on everything concerning me. I had the nerve to get offended when family members thought she had me under a spell. They were believing that every decision I made was prompted by her; like I couldn't think for myself. I didn't see it then, but looking back I can see how they would think that. I really did value her opinion and my hunger for truth had me vulnerable. She was the one that God had sent to advise and support me. She was the one that opened her home and her heart to guide me. However, I wasn't aware of the toll that it was really taking on her. This was a big job to handle. Kingdom work is not easy. I admire her for her strength and her resilience. It must have felt to her like I was one of her children. She had 6 children and a newborn granddaughter at this time. I was child number 7. The task she had taken on to mentor me was fragile. Leading someone to Christ is a delicate matter. You are literally responsible for someone else's life. Now I can see why sometimes she was very careful in what she would say to me. Sometimes it would seem like she was confused. I would be wondering why she would never give me a straight answer. Now I realize that she couldn't. Certain things could only be revealed to me by God and some things I would have to learn through trial and error.

Chapter Eight

The Turning Point

*I*t is now 2014 and I am getting used to my new life. I'm not meeting with my relative every day, but we make sure we talk daily. We wanted to stretch ourselves more, so we decided to incorporate a New Testament Bible study plan into our regime. We began January 12, 2014 with the book of Acts. We started in Acts first because I understood that the book of Acts tells the importance of being obedient to God's Word and the transformation that occurs as a result of knowing Christ. That's what I needed to know. I was ready to be transformed.

We would read a few chapters at a time and then get together once or twice a week, usually over the phone.

We would ask questions (it was usually me with the questions) or just talk about something that stood out in the verses. I must say that I truly enjoyed that experience. The bible isn't as difficult to understand if you earnestly ask the Holy Spirit to give you clarity. I looked forward to those phone calls that always ended in prayer. I can look back and see how God was developing me in yet another area of my spiritual life. He was getting me accustomed to reading and teaching me how to pray. In the past I really struggled in my prayer life, mainly because I was constantly comparing myself to how others prayed. I concluded that the more I prayed, the more comfortable I would be in prayer. We had completed reading all the way through Revelation by March of 2014. I was becoming confident in leading prayer and I felt that I was getting closer to God. I still hadn't gotten to the point where I could say "God told me", but I knew that He was drawing me nearer.

My relative and I were a great team and I was ready to move in the things of God. If she was leading the way, I was on board to do my part. I had really come to admire her faith walk on a new level. I knew that God had led me here for a reason. I walked so close behind her to make sure I didn't miss a thing.

However, as time passed on, it seemed that the more eager I became, she became that much more evasive. I couldn't seem to get a straight answer from her about any-thing. When it came to organizing fellowships, we could never get the ball rolling. Whenever I asked her about it, she would only respond "I'm not sure" or "I'm waiting on God to tell me what to do and when to move." I don't know what she was dealing with, but it was frustrating me and I began to withdraw. Again.

My relative must have felt the tension building between us and she began calling more. I welcomed the gesture and we started hanging out again. In our efforts to deepen our quest for God, my relative and I and her family, began to fellowship at a home-based ministry. I had the pleasure of meeting the pastor's wife back in 2011. (another divine connection) I did not know what to expect, but I was looking forward to something other than the "church" experience that I had been used to. On the very first visit, we began with prayer, then praise and worship, and that's as far as we got. The Spirit of God was ushered in and totally took over. I had never felt the presence of God like that and I certainly had never been in a service where every person was engaged in the worship. There wasn't a dry eye in the place. Nobody was checking their phone, checking the time and nobody was dozing off. Some people were standing, some were kneeling, but we all were giving God praise. We were all on one accord. I couldn't even say it was a fluke because the same thing happened the next week and the next week and the week after that. Families were beginning to come with their kids. The kids were bringing their friends. I was looking forward to Sundays. This is the type of ministry that I believed would be the place to get me to another level so I joined.

This brought some tension between my relative and I, but I felt that God led me there for a reason and I had to be obedient to what I believed God was telling me to do; even if she didn't agree with it. The closer I grew to the Pastor's wife the further apart my relative and I became. The Pastor's wife was a mentor to me in so many ways. I was learning how to pray, how to hear God's voice and how to walk in faith. The time I spent under her wing, I grew tremendously. She really pushed me to levels I didn't know I could reach.

My reading and study time at home became more intense. I would just lay on the floor and cry out to God. It was during this time that God began to reveal to me just who I was and what was hindering our relationship. Sometimes during my sleep, the Holy Spirit would just whisper words to me. I would keep hearing it until I got up and wrote it down. By the time I finished writing, I had a complete poem written. For the next few weeks, I had to keep paper and pen in the bed with me because the Holy Spirit would wake me up in the middle of the night with more words. The real revelation came when I read back what I had written. Each poem that was written was about an event or incident from my past. Reading some of them brought me to tears. Staring at the words on the paper was like looking at myself in a mirror but a younger version of myself. I had laid my heart out in black and white. I was now able to see bitterness, rejection, pride, rebellion, and loneliness.(just to name a few) I began to remember things from the past that I had dismissed and placed into the deepest parts of my memory. Things that the younger Tori didn't know how to handle so she buried them.

Things that caused her to build a wall so tall and wide that no one could break through to get close. Not even God.

This part of my process was exceedingly difficult and draining. God had me in isolation during this period. I even had to break off communication with my relative with no explanation to her. My obedience in this phase was vital. I was so desperate to break down every wall and hindrance to get to the place that God was trying to get me to. I didn't care that people didn't understand what I was dealing with or why I was making the decisions I was making. I can honestly say that some of it didn't make sense to me either. I just knew that the Holy Spirit had put such an urgency in me that I became radically obedient. I began to renounce every negative thing that was revealed to me through the poems. Every time I read one, I felt a release. It was like a cleansing taking place. When the Holy Spirit finally gave me a break from the nightly visits, I had my first book completed. I titled it *"To God be the Glory"*.

The isolation period only lasted about a month, but it seemed like an eternity. Having this peek into my past released some memories that I believed God wanted me to explore. It was time for me to look back to the beginning where it all began.

Chapter Nine

Identity Crisis

Mother's baby, Daddy's maybe

They say that the first relationship a girl experiences with a man is with her father. That relationship was supposed to demonstrate or reflect on how I should expect to be treated by a man. They also say that girls who grow up without their fathers end up battling low self-esteem and, very often, feelings of unworthiness. Telling my story has caused me to evaluate my past and uncover the factors that played a part in molding me into the woman that I had become - broken, bitter, resentful and ashamed. In fact, I was living in denial about my low self-esteem. From my perspective, the reality of growing up without my biological father didn't appear to have created any major flaws in my character, if any at all. In fact, I believed it had no bearing at all. I didn't feel any sense of loss by his not being there. Even in the presence of other girls with their fathers, I didn't feel any type of way, at least, not in my conscious mind.

I did have an adult male figure in my life, though he was not my biological father. He and my mother lived together for over 20 years, and I never called him dad. My mom didn't ask me to do so, either. I never felt a real connection with him. Our relationship was ok, but not remarkably close. I don't recall any type of love being expressed between us. I felt as though I was just being tolerated because I was a package deal with my mom. A lot of times, I felt that I was just misunderstood. I knew that I was just a kid, but this man was not my daddy, and how come whatever he said was how it went? As I saw it, he wasn't good enough for my mom, and I didn't like the way he was always proving that he was in charge. No matter what was going on or what I would say, she would always take his side. I guess that was where some of the ill feelings that I felt toward him stemmed from.

God's plan was for each child to have two parents - a mother and a father. The dynamics of that family structure would then create an atmosphere of love, trust, and stability. For some reason, my life didn't play out like that.

I didn't have the nurturing father-daughter relationship that God intended for daughters to have. Like I said earlier, I didn't recognize that I was being neglected. Only in the knowledge that I have now and seeing the state that I was in, have I concluded something was missing, and that part of my life had a direct connection with the way I matured. I do understand now that although in my conscious mind, I didn't feel as though I missed out on anything, there was definitely something that a father imparts to his daughter that I was lacking.

I am my mother's only child and we had a good relationship. However, there is a connection and bond that can exist between a father and daughter that brings revelation to the daughter about her relationship with God. If a daughter has not experienced this type of connection, it may hinder her ability to accept and receive the love of God.

Just to sit here and recall these moments and hear from the Holy Spirit, is causing my heart to become full. I am recognizing that telling my story is a part of my healing process. Having the Holy Spirit walk with me through these feelings and moments that may have been detrimental to my emotional state, is actually God's way of helping me to release those hardened memories that were hindering my growth without causing any further damage. Thank you, Jesus.

Shades of Blackness

I grew up in the 60's and 70's. Back then, there was a clear discrimination amongst black people who joined in the never-ending divide between being "light-skinned" and "dark-skinned". If you were light-skinned, you were automatically considered cute. If you were dark-skinned then you were not so cute. It's absurd, but that's sadly how it was. It still happens in today's society, but not as much as it did back in the day. I was the dark-skinned girl. I had friends that I spent a lot of time with who were all light-skinned, who also had the "special feature" of what was considered to be "good" hair. I loved spending time with my friends, however, I often felt that I was treated as less than they were. I always assumed it was because of the tone of my skin. It may or may not have been and I'll never be sure, but I felt the indifference. I believed I was always being compared to them.

During high school, I had several bouts with seborrhea; a form of eczema that affects the scalp. In those times, my hair fell out in some areas leaving the only option to cut all of my hair to the length of the shortest parts. I had to wash with a special shampoo for about 2 weeks, but it took much longer for the hair to grow back. Can you imagine my self-esteem then? Not only was my hair "nappy", now I'm what they called "picky-headed". There were people to tell me that I was beautiful, but I never believed them. I didn't think that I was beautiful. I couldn't see what they saw.

I would describe myself as average looking, not weight/ height appropriate, but a little thickness with an okay shape. I don't usually stand out in a crowd; I'm more of the background type. You might accidentally bump into me on your way to the bathroom. Nevertheless, I do okay when it comes to attracting the opposite sex. I have had my share of the "boy if you don't get outta my face" encounters, but never the one that I could run home and tell momma about. It seemed that the girls around me were getting all of the attention of the "good ones". I just couldn't understand it. Usually if one of the "good ones" approached me, it was to ask me to "hook them up with my girl". I'm sure wondering, "What in the world does she have that I don't and what is she doing that I'm not?" I have always been the shy type, but even us shy girls need love. I wanted so badly to just come out and ask my girls, "what is your secret?" but never had the courage to. I heard rumors about them "putting out" but I knew better. My two best friends, Niecy and Ashley always had some guy drooling behind them. I know for a fact that they were not putting out because we made a pact while in high school, that we would tell each other when we were ready to "do it". Niecy was fine and beautiful. She was light skinned, had pretty light brown eyes and had that "good hair" and a coke bottle shape. I mean, she had it going on and she knew it. She would have the guys running behind her, stalking her and she would just dismiss them like old news when she was through with them. She had it like that.

Once she was done with them, she wouldn't give them the time of day. I was usually left making excuses and trying to comfort the poor fellow of the week. Ashley wasn't as fine as Niecy, but she was slim, had long hair and she was cute. She also carried herself like she was all that and a bag of chips. I guess that could be something that they had that I didn't. Remember, I was the dark skinned one of the group and I sure didn't have the confidence they had.

Ball of Confusion

I was raised Catholic and attended Catholic schools. That was considered a good thing back then. I now know some of the sacrifices my mom made so that I could attend a private school. However, I was not taught about having a relationship with God. I didn't know there was even such a thing. I don't even recall having a bible at home as I grew up. At church, we didn't even have to open the bible, because we had what you would call a missalette. All the prayers and everything we needed for mass, was printed in that booklet. After so long, I didn't need the pamphlet because it was always the same thing every week. I knew there was a God and something about a holy trinity. If you did something wrong, you would have to go to confession. I think you could only go once a month or once a week, I'm not sure, but there was a specific time for it. Usually, after you confessed to the priest, you would be asked to go to the altar and say the Hail Mary twice, Our Father once and the Act of Contrition once or some combination of those prayers and all was forgiven. I was taught early how to go through the motions, doing a thing without really knowing what I was doing or why. The closest you could get to God was talking to the priest. I was left with the impression that God was like the wizard of Oz. If I didn't find the yellow brick road, I wouldn't find him. To me, it felt like too much to go through with no surety that I would even reach him. So why try? The idea of a relationship with God was nonexistent.

I don't even recall my mother ever going to church with me or even at all. I do remember walking to church with my cousins and friends from the neighborhood. There came a time when I only pretended to go to church. Instead, a few of us from the neighborhood would hang out in the grocery store across from the church. We would keep an eye out for the people coming out of the church to know when it was time to go home.

As an adult, I have had a conversation with my mom about growing up Catholic and she explained to me why she did not attend church. The Catholic Church believes that sex was created by God to express love and commitment from one spouse to another. Furthermore, sex outside of marriage isn't what God intended and for a couple to engage in such activity was against the Catholic standard. Doing so would denote deception because the couple does not have what the Catholic Church considered a total commitment; that being a marriage. She felt she was living in sin by living with a man she was not married to and going to church would label her as a hypocrite. Then, she told me something that brought some light to a dark area in my life. It may seem trivial, but it brought clarity to some things that God had revealed to me since I have been on this journey. There were two reasons why she didn't want to get married or have children with the man she lived with for so many years. The first reason was she didn't want me to have a different last name than she did. Ok. That's understandable. Now the second reason is the one that got me in my feelings. She was fearful that if they had children they would be born with light skin and light-colored eyes. Hmmm? Does this sound familiar? So maybe it wasn't my imagination about the differential treatment I believed I received. My mother was trying to protect me from something. My God! I love how God is bringing healing through this process. I feel that this is a breakthrough in my relationship with my mother as well. Things I didn't understand back then, God is now bringing revelation to it.

Nevertheless, in all of the church-going and prayers and kneeling and confessing in the catholic church, I was not any closer to finding out who God was. I had missing pieces and broken parts that I wasn't even aware of.

Chapter Ten

Eyes Wide Open

I had brought in the new year of 2015 at the home-based ministry, with Malcolm praying with me over the phone. I was embarking upon my second year of being in Columbus and I had been expecting God to bring Malcolm and I back together. I realized that there was still more work to be done. I had been spending more and more time in prayer and even more time just sitting in God's presence. I was at a pivotal point in my life and I wanted to go beyond where God had already taken me. I knew that there was more for me and I knew that God had something specific for me to do. So far, I had broken away from what was familiar, in order for me to launch into the next level of my truth being revealed. I had found out that I was more than I believed I was, and that God had given me gifts and talents to use for His glory.

My next venture would entail some revelation, deliverance, and purging. The home-based ministry had really embraced me and was pulling me into a deeper experience with God. The pastor's wife had become more of a mentor to me and we began to spend a lot of time together. I really wanted to understand what it was she saw in me, and I wanted to know what I needed to do to allow God to use me. I had been told years ago that I would be the catalyst that would draw my family to God. I had already been separated from them for 2 years at this point. I refused to let the naysayers have the last word, so I pressed on.

That's right. Can you believe that some were even expecting that I would fail miserably and have to come crawling back to Louisiana. Some people literally spoke against my marriage. I knew that God had spoken to me and I had to continue to trust Him at His word. He is not a man that He should lie, and I truly believed that with all of my heart. Even on my worst day, I still had to be convinced that it would work out for my good. I couldn't give up, because so much depended on me.

Through spending time with the pastor's wife, I was able to grasp what it meant to have faith in God. I would see her in a situation that could normally send someone over the edge, but she held on, trusting God to see it through. God allowed me to be that up close and personal to see Him come through in a time of need.

I began practicing my faith and speaking the word of God over myself and my situation and I started seeing more evidence little by little. I began hearing God speaking to me in my dreams. I would wake up in the middle of the night to write something that He said. Sometimes, it would be the title of a poem. Sometimes, it would be a scripture. Sometimes, it would even be a whole verse to a poem. What was so amazing about the whole thing was, after I would complete the poem and read it back, it would be a revelation about a time of struggle in my life. Some of it I remembered, but some of it I had buried deep in my memory and had forgotten that it even took place. Each poem that I was writing was actually bringing up those things that were hindering my growth. Things that I had not accepted about myself or my past that I had allowed to block God from totally entering in. Sometimes, I couldn't wait to get to sleep to see what God was going to share with me next. I learned that I was bitter, resentful, rebellious, insecure, and I had low self-esteem. I learned that I had not totally forgiven Malcolm, as I thought I had. I also learned that I had not forgiven myself. I sure did a lot of crying after reading those poems. I also realized that each poem released the enemy's hold on me and freed me to be open to receive more of God's love for me. God was able to come closer to me and to fill those spaces that had been void. Those places that I had been expecting Malcolm to fill. I was made aware of the pressure I had placed on my marriage by my unrealistic expectations.

Third Sundays at the home-based ministry was set aside for testimonies and expressions from anyone who wanted to share. I began sharing my poetry. Even though I had written the poetry and read it at home, when I got up to share with the ministry, it brought even more healing to me. I saw that others were being healed and encouraged by it. I was beginning to see what God wanted me to do with my gift. I was beginning to understand how writing could be used for God's glory.

When I began to look at the work of poetry I had done, I was able to see my transformation. In my earlier writings, I could definitely see the bitterness and sarcasm. I could see that I was hurt and wanted to get revenge on whoever it was that hurt me. I couldn't physically do it, so I would put it on paper. I wrote about significant events in my life that sculpted my character. All of those feelings had me bound into a negative mindset. I didn't trust anyone. I wouldn't let anyone get too close to me for fear that they would hurt me. Most times, my thinking was I was going to get you before you got me. I was very smart mouthed and every word that came out of my mouth was spewing venom. I could see why some people would tiptoe around me while others were even hesitant to approach me. I wore it on my face and didn't even know it.

Oh, but I thank God that He loves me the way He does. He brought me all the way to Columbus, Georgia where it would be just me and Him. He knew what He had put in me and it was time for it to be brought out; for all of the masks to be removed. I understand why my relative and I had to be separated now. I know she probably doesn't understand yet, but by the time this book is released, we will have begun doing the work of the Lord together as He said years ago.

I believe many of you can attest to this. The enemy gets very upset when things are going right in your life so he has to try to intervene. Sure enough in the midst of my eyes being opened and being delivered, the enemy tried to scare me with sickness. In the middle of the night I would wake up feeling nauseous, feeling faint, not being able to breathe. I was feeling like I was having a heart attack. I really thought I was going to die. I would get up and walk up and down the hallway praying, praising God, and rebuking the enemy in Jesus' name. I would tell God that I knew He didn't bring me this far to leave me. A few times, I called the pastor's wife and she reminded me that what I was going through was spiritual and that I had to ask God to rebuke the enemy and to continue to give God the praise. This went on every other night for about 2 or 3 weeks. It was so hard at times and it felt like it wasn't ever going to end. As I fought more in the spiritual realm through prayer, the sick feeling would subside. I had come to know how to fight the enemy. God was definitely preparing me for things to come.

I saw my prayer life thriving and my prayer language flourishing. I was getting bolder at church. I wasn't just a "pew warmer." I was up praising God. I was engaged in every aspect of the service. I saw God using me to shift the atmosphere in prayer in the ministry.

By March of 2015, I was another 15 lbs. lighter and a dress size smaller. Another mask had fallen off. God was truly doing a makeover on me. I could look in the mirror at myself and see a beautiful woman. I was liking what God was doing in me and this new found confidence was refreshing.

In this phase of my transition, God gave me an opportunity to get to know myself. I had to be comfortable enough within myself to be able to need people without being needy. I understand that God was teaching me to embrace being alone without feeling lonely. In fact, being in the will of God assured me that I was never totally alone, because He is always with me.

I utilized the extra free time, focusing on my writing more. I knew that the book was a major part of God's plan and being secluded was God's way of making sure I was hearing Him as I was writing. I had planned to write the book about one thing when God began redirecting me. I had to literally sleep with my pen and notebook in bed with me. God would speak to me in my dreams so vividly that I would be driven to wake and write. I tried to wait until I got up a few times, but by the time I did, the words were gone. I learned that I had to write as He was speaking to me. I definitely had to do it His way.

I would go through moments of fluidity, where I was writing every day, sometimes all day, to moments of silence. God is wise like that. He knows not to give me too much at a time. I was made sure to know that it was all Him; that I was writing the book as He led. Now I don't get frustrated in those dry times. I acknowledge that God is giving me time to grasp everything. He doesn't want me or allow me to get overwhelmed.

I love God's pace. His timing. Everything about me has evolved - my mindset, what makes me happy, what can and cannot move me. I am a better woman because of it.

At each level of my transformation, He was purging me of all my brokenness, removing the masks one by one, and in every breath I took, he was breathing in more of His virtue. As I grew into my new self, I was better equipped to help someone else who was in a similar situation. Two broken people can't carry each other. I was learning that the hard way.

I am in no way proclaiming that this is an easy task. However, I am saying that it is able to be done. God wouldn't expect us to do anything that He has not already equipped us to do. If He tells you to do it, trust that you can. I am learning to surrender daily. Everything about surrendering has to do with making a conscious decision to do the will of God. It's a choice and I chose God.

Chapter Eleven

A New Me in Town

*I*n July 2015, I took a trip to Louisiana. I was feeling more confident than I had ever felt and I even felt beautiful. When you truly surrender to God, He will do a new thing for sure in your life. Not only internally, but I believed He restored a look of youthfulness to me that I can't explain. Some people didn't even recognize me immediately. When I walked away from one group of people, I felt like Loretta Devine in *"Waiting to Exhale"* when she was walking away from Gregory Hines. For sure, when I turned around, they were looking and scratching their heads; like, was that Tori?

In my new-found confidence, I found myself responding differently. Times when I would normally not speak up, I was speaking up. Then there were times when I would normally cause a raucous and I was calm. I was totally proud of the woman I had become, and I could see that some people (family) were surprised about the changes that had taken place in me. They were finally given the opportunity to see upfront what God had been doing in me since I left. I was walking taller, speaking with assurance, and looking like I had a complete makeover. I purposely didn't dabble too long in anyone's presence, because God wasn't through with me yet. I was just there to handle business and get back to Columbus. I wasn't quite ready to be "fully unveiled". Some people may have felt slighted, mainly Malcolm, but I was being obedient to the directions that the Lord had given me. I know that when I left, a lot was on his mind about this new wife of his. He was certainly looking at me differently; I suspect it was in a good way.

When I got back to Columbus, I felt like another weight had been lifted off my shoulders and another layer of mask was beginning to fall away. But it was only round one. There was more fighting to be done. There was more preparation to be done. God was strategically freeing me from my past. He was stripping away every old mindset, bad habit and every other thing that was not like him. He was giving me lesson by lesson, step by step. After each lesson was a test. I learned that the test doesn't always come exactly like the lesson. God was teaching me how to study so well as to recognize the test no matter how it came. I can honestly say that I didn't pass a few of the tests. Some tests came disguised as a blessing. I had been praying for discernment.

I had been asking God to show me when someone was trying to deceive me. I wanted to be able to recognize when the enemy was trying to do a sneak attack. I thank God for His mercy and grace that He extends to us especially when He knows that we are diligently seeking Him and attempting to be in His will. I know that I had a long way to go, but I also knew that I had come a long way. The old Tori was slowly fading to nothingness and the new creation was evolving.

I began growing and expanding, like the caterpillar in its second stage of transformation, called the larvae. As I was soaking in everything that the Lord was showing me, I began growing and expanding. With the caterpillar, their skin doesn't stretch or grow, so they begin molting. This means that they shed the outgrown skin several times throughout that stage. That's what I was doing. The more I read, the more I studied, the more I prayed, the more I fasted. I was shedding the old layers and growing into the beauty that God created me to be.

Chapter Twelve

Hope for tomorrow

oliday season is my favorite time of the year. This time last year was not a time to be remembered. As much as I love giving and sharing during the holidays, I was very much alone. This year was different. I had a little money from a settlement, and I was in a very giving mood. I was hoping and praying that this would be the season of change, especially in my marriage. My husband and I were trying to be on the same page about it all, and we were getting close to a breakthrough. He was coming in for the holidays, and I was excited to do something extra special for him.

In the past, Malcolm was always the one doing the gift giving. I rarely recall, if ever, that Malcolm received anything from anybody. He would say that he didn't want to receive anything, but I believe that was to ease his expectations for when he actually didn't receive anything. I knew it made him feel some type of way to always be the one that everyone would go to when they needed something and when the opportunity came for them to possibly do something for him, it never happened.

The more I prayed about our situation, the more God revealed to me about Malcolm. He began showing me what to pray for. He showed me things about Malcolm that Malcolm never talked to me about. I began to see Malcolm from a different perspective. I was beginning to understand more about "the man" as I looked at him as God sees him. I was able to look past the exterior wall that he built up and see into his heart. I felt his pain. I saw his disappointments, his fears, his insecurities. God trusted me with that information, not to use it against Malcolm, but to pray about it. Before I knew it, I was falling in love all over again.

I was so excited about the new love I was experiencing. I took Christmas shopping to another level. In the beginning, I wasn't thinking about doing any shopping, but I felt in my heart that I needed to do something really special for Malcolm. He was coming in for Christmas and I wanted him to know what it's like to unwrap gifts for Christmas. When I was done shopping, I had to call in for help with the gift wrapping. I had a gift-wrapping party at my place. Thank God for friends.

I had put up a tree but decided not to place the gifts there just yet. I hid them under the bed in the guest room. Right at midnight, I was able to get to the bedroom and place the gifts under the tree. I called Malcolm into the living room while video recording. As he walked in, all he could say was "Woowwwww!" He looked like a little boy as he opened each gift one by one. The last gift was a diamond wedding band. I don't know what that experience was really like for him but I know how it made me feel to do that for him. I felt that we really bonded during that time and I was hopeful for a change. Not long after he returned home, things became silent again.

Chapter Thirteen

Growing Pains

At some point, I stopped to look back and saw just how far I had come. I was shouting and thanking God for my progress and growth. I was at a place that I didn't perceive as possible for me. I was doing things that I would never in a million years see myself doing. I was hearing God. I was trusting God. I was seeing prayers being manifested. I threw a quick celebration for myself in my mind. After that short celebration, I turned back around and had no clue where I was. I was staring straight ahead into darkness with no clear sign of what was ahead. That's how fast you can get off track. God quickly showed me that I still had a long way to go. He wanted to make sure that I didn't get too far ahead of myself, and more importantly, ahead of Him. I was quickly reminded that I will never be perfect, and I won't make it until I make it. Praise God. The work that God had begun in me will continue until the day of Jesus Christ. This flesh that my spirit dwells in will make sure of that. No matter how far I go, this flesh of mine will steadily have a hold of me, trying to pull me back. It is up to me to feed my spirit daily to ensure that my flesh will never overtake me to bring me under. That dark place that I found myself in was evidence that the enemy was right on my tail. I realized that I didn't have time to stop and celebrate too long or he would certainly catch up to me. I knew that the closer I got to Jesus, the harder I would have to fight, pray, and dig deeper. That revelation got my mind right. I had gotten comfortable; again. I had subconsciously let go of God's hand and was wondering why I was feeling lost. The things that I had done to get to this place were surely not going to be enough to sustain me in this new level of relationship. Greater levels require greater sacrifices. The journey to the promised land can be as smooth or as hard as our level of faith and our commitment to being obedient to the word and plan of God. Where God was trying to bring me, I would have to prove that I was totally submitted and committed before He would plant me there. No matter how much I believed in my heart and spoke out of my mouth, it wouldn't mean a thing until my mindset changed and my actions confirmed it. I knew that God was working on me and that some obvious changes had taken place but this next phase was going to make the difference in the entire purpose of my journey. I was still saying I, when I knew that it wasn't about me. I know that the decisions and choices I make today will affect my children, my children's children, and several generations after that. That is one thing that we were not taught to consider back when I was growing up. The world is all about self and the momentary gratification from feeding the flesh. The more I sought God, the wider and clearer my perception was becoming. Although I was in a constant battle with my mind, I knew that I had the power of the Holy Spirit in me to take control and make the better, wiser decision than to settle for the choice that would make me feel good right now. God is looking for the one with self integrity. The one who could be honest with themselves about who they are. The one that would do what was right even if no one was looking. But that's the thing. Somehow, we tend to forget that God is watching. He sees everything. He is the one important person that should make it matter to us. I guess it takes time for us to get to that level of understanding our relationship with God, where we are convicted by our immoral behavior and it becomes intolerable for us to remain in that state. I'm not sure if it was sooner or later for me, but I did begin to realize that some things that I was used to doing just were not conducive to my new lifestyle and mindset. I had a fear of God that would not permit me to do them. I had a love and respect for God that I didn't want to disappoint Him. This is how I truly knew that I was growing.

Chapter Fourteen

Full Circle

The next year and a half went by quickly. It is now 2017. I'm loving the new woman I have become and I have learned so much about the character of God and how wonderful He is. My biggest challenge was still dealing with my husband and our marriage, but I hung on to God's promise of restoration. Although we were still separated and things did not look good on the surface, I believed in my heart that God was going to turn things around. Malcolm was always trying to reassure me that he was working things out and that we would get things back on track. I understood that Malcolm had good intentions, but his pride, stubbornness and impulsiveness usually led him in a different direction. I had placed my faith in him many times in the past only to be let down again. One thing I learned was that God would never let me down. God is the only one that I can lean on and trust.

The next thing that happened caused me to put my money where my mouth was. One of my children had become sick. In the beginning we were thinking it was the flu. He was having chills but no fever. Like he always did, he just took some Nyquil. That was his go to medicine for whatever he was dealing with. After a few weeks of not getting better, he went to the emergency room near his apartment. He was told he had walking pneumonia. He was given some cough medicine and some antibiotics to take. After about a week of that, he got worse. He called me to bring him a few things. While I was there, I tried to talk him into going back to the hospital. Instead, he agreed to come stay with me so I could help him until he got better. He continued getting worse to the point where he struggled to breathe when he exerted himself.

This was on a Sunday evening and on Monday morning he finally agreed to let me take him to the hospital. They admitted him and warfare began. He went from bad to worse in a matter of days and I told God He had to step in. The Holy Spirit in me kept my head clear and I remained calm; on the outside. I was praying over him constantly and I was listening intently to the leading of the Holy Spirit. After two months of being connected to a ventilator, I watched my son take his last breath. That was the hardest thing I have ever had to do in my life. I know that if it had not been for what God had been doing in me, I would have been a basket case. Through the instructions that God gave me concerning my son, I know that he was in God's hands. I prayed strategic prayers and intercessors were praying with me. My son knew that he was loved, and I believe he was at peace. He had an experience with God right there in the hospital.

God is so deliberate and intentional. He plans things and we have no clue why He has us doing certain things. Therefore, we must strive to be obedient to his commands. He knows what things we will face and what we will need to get through them. Everything was in place.

And just as suddenly as I was led by the Holy Spirit to leave Louisiana, I was being directed to head back. I know that God doesn't make any mistakes, but I'm asking God, "Are you sure?" The nerve of me. Deep down, I knew that it was in order. I have had numerous opportunities and requests to come back home, but somehow, this time, I felt the urgency that now was the time. This time, I knew that it was God for sure. Of course, I needed my confirmation as usual. I prayed about it and I fasted and then prayed again. On the last day of my fast and right after I prayed, I received a text that simply read, "God says the answer is yes." In radical obedience, I once again packed my bags and stepped out in faith.

From the Author

To my family and friends that didn't understand why I was making such a sudden move, I pray that this sheds some light on my decision. I can imagine some saying I should not have left. If they were me, they wouldn't have left their husband. They didn't know that my husband was in deeper than Larry Fishburne in the movie Deep Cover. Those of you who have seen the movie know exactly how deep I'm talking. I didn't recognize my husband anymore. He was beginning to live the lie as the truth and I had become the other woman. I knew there was nothing that I, nor anybody else could do or say to bring us back to reality. Nobody but God.

Contrary to popular belief, the reasoning behind my leaving wasn't totally about him, it was about my sanity and my soul being saved. It was God's way of getting my attention off my situation and to focus totally on Him. He was trying to reveal to me who I was and what my purpose was. I honestly believe that if I had stayed, I would have died spiritually for sure, and then who knows how far it would have gone after that. Often, we perpetrate the crime against ourselves, by delving too much into a mate or partner or other things, that we take away the necessary time and the ability to get to know God and even ourselves. We get so deeply entangled into those things that we commit a spiritual and emotional suicide. That thing that God was trying to birth out of me would never have a chance to be born and the relationship that I now have with Him would be non-existent.

At the end of the day, we are all responsible for our own salvation. No one can accept it for us no matter how hard they try. I had to stop trying to force my husband to change his life just because I was trying to change mine. When I stand before God in judgment, He wouldn't ask me a thing about my husband. I would be held accountable for my own actions and he would be responsible for his. On the other hand, because he was the head, God would question my husband about why he was out of position and why his family was broken.

I also understood that renewing my mind was going to be a daily process. It's a very conscientious acclamation that has to take place. When the enemy has a hold of you, he is holding on for keeps. So, if you're not fighting, you will stay bound. I promise it won't be easy, but what good thing is easy to come by? Oh, but if you endure, you can win! "The battle is not given to the swift, but to the one who can endure." I was determined to endure. The more the devil fought me and threw up roadblocks, I just went to God to re-load. I began to fight in the spirit instead of trying to fight in the physical realm. As it concerned my marriage, I came to a point when I stopped talking. I stopped pleading and I stopped trying to reason and make sense of it all. I had finally realized that I was in a spiritual battle that had to be fought in just that way--spiritually.

I don't understand why it took me so long to get there, but I am so grateful that God didn't allow me to stay stuck where I was. I am grateful that He had surrounded me with people that understood that God provides purpose for the lives of His people. They understood the kinds of holds the enemy can place upon us and the lies he tells us. They understood that we need each other to be like-minded and on one accord to defeat the new way of thinking and see-ing things. I was seeing things as God saw them because I had removed the masks. He connected me with people that loved Him and were seeking Him daily. In turn, they nur-tured me, taught me, labored with me, prayed with me and guided me until I came to the place that I am now. Neither of us saw it coming, but God does it like that. You will just look back one day and say "Wow! How did I get here?" My mind had been renewed and I had a new way of thinking and seeing things. I was seeing things as God saw them because I had removed the masks.

Made in the USA
Columbia, SC
14 March 2024

32736007R00046